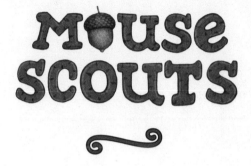

MOUSE SCOUTS

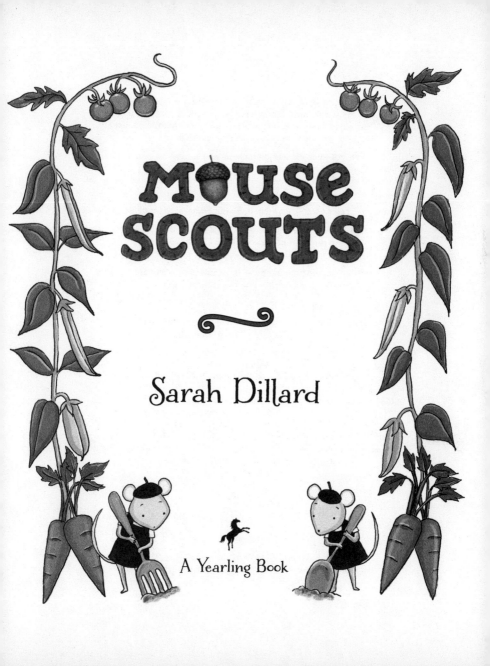

MOUSE SCOUTS

Sarah Dillard

A Yearling Book

Copyright © 2016 by Sarah Dillard
Melody for *The Acorn Scout Song* by Frank Fighera, lyrics by Sarah Dillard

All rights reserved. Published in the United States by Yearling,
an imprint of Random House Children's Books,
a division of Penguin Random House LLC, New York.

Yearling and the jumping horse design are registered trademarks
of Penguin Random House LLC.

Visit us on the Web! randomhousekids.com

Educators and librarians, for a variety of teaching tools, visit us at
RHTeachersLibrarians.com

Library of Congress Cataloging-in-Publication Data
Dillard, Sarah.
Mouse Scouts / Sarah Dillard. — First edition.
pages cm.
Summary: To earn their Sow It and Grow It badge, Violet, Tigerlily, and the
other Mouse Scouts plant a vegetable garden.
ISBN 978-0-385-75599-3 (trade) — ISBN 978-0-385-75600-6 (lib. bdg.) —
ISBN 978-0-385-75602-0 (trade pbk.) — ISBN 978-0-385-75601-3 (ebook)
[1. Scouting (Youth activity)—Fiction. 2. Vegetable gardening—Fiction.
3. Gardening—Fiction. 4. Mice—Fiction.] I. Title.
PZ7.D57733Mo 2015
[Fic]—dc23
2014001030

Printed in the United States of America
10 9 8 7 6 5 4 3 2 1
First Yearling Edition 2016

For Lori Nowicki

Contents

CHAPTER 1

Violet and Tigerlily

Violet placed her acorn cap on her head. It made her forehead itch and her ears stick out, but that didn't matter. She was finally going to be an Acorn Scout! She had been waiting for this moment her *whole* life. Now she just had to wait for Tigerlily and they'd be on their way to their first meeting.

Violet and Tigerlily had been best friends since the first day of Buttercups. Violet was the quietest mouse at the meeting, and Tigerlily could not sit still. Miss Primrose, the Buttercup leader, made

them sit together. "Maybe you'll rub off on each other," she said. They didn't, but Violet thought Tigerlily was funny, and Tigerlily loved making Violet laugh.

But Buttercups was for little mice, and they were big mice now. Last week, they had had the Butterfly ceremony, which was when the Buttercups moved up to the next level of Scouting. Violet had been nervous because the ceremony involved live butterflies. *Eek!* But with Tigerlily's help, she got through it. And now they were Acorns. Or they *would* be if Tigerlily would only hurry up and get here already.

Violet's nose twitched, as it always did when she was nervous. "What if Tigerlily doesn't make it? What if we're late?"

Violet had heard that Miss Poppy, the Acorn Scout leader, was very strict. There were rumors that she had once sent a Mouse Scout back to Buttercups for forgetting the words to the Mouse Scout pledge. Getting sent back to Buttercups would be horrible. Being a Buttercup last year was fine, but the thought of having to sing the Buttercup song one more time made her shudder. And while Violet loved art and was very crafty, she had had enough of flower-petal collages. She was ready for new experiences.

Violet's thoughts were interrupted by a loud *thwack! Thwack*s were never a good thing. The last time she'd heard that sound, her fellow Buttercup Petunia had sprung a mousetrap. She had barely escaped.

Her tail would be crooked for the rest of her life. Violet started. "Oh no! Tigerlily!" Then she relaxed. If anyone knew their way around a mousetrap, it was Tigerlily.

Sure enough, a few seconds later, Tigerlily squeezed through Violet's front door.

Her acorn cap was already crooked and her uniform was wrinkled. "Yuck," she said, holding up a piece of cheese. "It's dried-up Gorgonzola. It's been a long time since anyone has bothered with that trap. You don't have any cheddar, do you?"

"Tigerlily!" Violet squeaked. "This is no time for cheese. We'll never make it. We're going to be late. Miss Poppy will send us back to Buttercups. *I can't go back to Buttercups!*"

"No problem," said Tigerlily. "I know a shortcut."

"Really?" Violet was suspicious. She knew about Tigerlily's shortcuts.

"Honest!" said Tigerlily. "We'll be there in no time!"

The shortcut took longer than Violet

would have liked, but as Tigerlily prom-
ised, they slipped into the basement of the
Left Meadow Elementary School with a
minute to spare.

MOUSE SCOUT HANDBOOK

THE ACORN SCOUT

Now you are an Acorn Scout!

The Acorn

Acorns are important to mice. Not only are they wonderful to eat—try roasting them or grinding them into flour to make acorn pancakes—they are also used for bowls and cups.

But the acorn is much more than that! It is a powerful symbol of knowledge and growth. Just as the tiny acorn will one day be a mighty oak tree, you are beginning a journey to becoming a great Mouse Scout!

When you meet other Mouse Scouts, always

greet them with the Mouse Scout salute followed by the sign of the Acorn. This way you will be recognized as a Scout and accepted as a friend. Little Buttercups will look to you for guidance, while older Sunflower Scouts will help you whenever you need it.

SIGN OF THE ACORN

STEP 1   STEP 2

The Mouse Scout Pledge

On my honor as an Acorn,
I promise to be
trustworthy and strong,
thrifty and brave,
and helpful to all in need.

The Acorn Scout Song

We are Acorns, tiny and small.
But we'll grow up to be mighty and tall.
We're quick with a plan,
and we help when we can.
We love our friends and are kind to all.

CHAPTER 2

The Summer Project

Violet and Tigerlily were the last to arrive. Miss Poppy looked at them. She was even scarier than Violet had imagined. *Please don't send me back to Buttercups, please don't send me back to Buttercups,* she thought.

Miss Poppy cleared her throat. "Before we start, I want to remind

everyone that this is not Buttercups any-
more. You are Acorns. Tardiness will not
be tolerated. Now let's all recite the Mouse
Scout pledge."

Violet breathed for the first time since
entering the room and joined the other
Scouts in reciting the pledge.

> *On my honor as an Acorn,*
> *I promise to be*
> *trustworthy and strong,*
> *thrifty and brave,*
> *and helpful to all in need.*

After the pledge, Miss Poppy went over
a few business matters.

"Acorns meet weekly in this space at this
time. As I have mentioned, I expect punc-

tuality. Meetings will consist of reciting the pledge, reviewing any business matters that need attention, occasional short presentations on specified themes, and crafts and activities. We will close each meeting with the singing of the Acorn Scout song. You are expected to help tidy our area before you leave. In addition, this summer we will be working on a large project, which I will introduce later in this meeting. This project will require us to spend extra time beyond the scope of the weekly meetings, which you are still expected to attend. If you successfully participate in this project, you will earn a badge. Remember, badges are awarded on merit. You have to be present, and you have to participate. Be sure to study your *Mouse Scout Handbook* for proper care and cleaning of your Mouse Scout uniform. Wear your uniform to all Mouse Scout functions. When you take it off, brush it and hang it properly. Your uniform consists of your acorn cap, your neck scarf, which has many useful purposes besides decorative, your sash . . ."

Violet started to take notes, but her mind wandered as Miss Poppy droned on and on. Violet looked around the room at the other Scouts. She already knew everyone from Buttercups. Tigerlily was fidgeting beside her. Hyacinth looked bored, but her uniform was crisp and perfect.

Petunia was carefully
hiding her crooked tail.

Cricket had a few
crumbs in her lap, which
she nibbled on when
she thought no one was
looking.

Junebug sniffled
and reached in her
sleeve for a small
piece of tissue.

Violet caught Tigerlily's eye and smiled. No one was listening to Miss Poppy.

"THWEEEEEEET!"

Violet jumped out of her seat. She had never been so scared in her life! When she could finally breathe again, she glanced around the room. Everyone was sitting up straight with stunned looks on their faces.

Miss Poppy smiled. "THAT is your emergency whistle, which you should wear at all times. This was a demonstration only. Do NOT use your whistle unless there is an emergency. Repeated use of the whistle can be damaging to your ears.

It will be GLORIOUS!

"Now that we've covered that, it is time to move on. The special project I mentioned will be creating and maintaining a vegetable garden, working toward the 'Sow It and Grow It' badge. It will be GLORIOUS!"

Violet couldn't believe her luck. She had wanted to start a vegetable garden ever since she read the section "Acorn Scouts and Self-Sufficiency" in her *Mouse Scout Handbook*. She could see herself in a garden. She wanted it more than anything.

Tigerlily thought it was a horrible idea.

As far as she was concerned, gardening was hot, itchy, hard work. She wanted no part of it. Besides, she didn't even like vegetables.

"Your assignment for this afternoon is to scavenge for seeds," said Miss Poppy. "Report back here with them tomorrow morning, and we will begin our garden."

MOUSE SCOUT HANDBOOK

YOUR VEGETABLE GARDEN

Starting a Vegetable Garden: Introduction

For most mice, food comes from cupboards, countertops, and the occasional nut scavenged from the forest. But have you ever thought of growing food yourself? Nothing is as satisfying as starting a vegetable garden. Imagine serving your family a stuffed Brussels sprout or a cherry tomato roast that you prepared from vegetables you grew from seed. Your family will appreciate your hard work as they delight in meals made from your bountiful harvest.

And best of all, gardening is easy! All you need is dirt, some seeds, water, sunshine, and patience. Your summer will be filled with excitement as you watch nature at work. Before your eyes, you will see a bare piece of ground transform into a luxuriant garden.

CHAPTER 3

Seed Safari

After the meeting, the Mouse Scouts lingered outside of the Left Meadow Elementary School.

"I've never been so bored," said Hyacinth.

"Me neither," said Petunia. She was always trying to be just like Hyacinth.

"She's not like Miss Primrose," Tigerlily said. Miss Primrose had been cuddly and kind . . . everything Miss Poppy was not.

Violet agreed with Tigerlily. She thought Miss Poppy was scary. But the meeting was over, and they had work to do.

"Where do we get seeds?" she asked.

"There are usually some seeds by the bagel bin," said Cricket. She lived in the grocery store and always had great snacks.

"Wrong kind of seeds, unless we want to grow poppy and sesame bagels," said Hyacinth. "We need *vegetable* seeds."

"Sesame isn't even a plant, is it?" asked Tigerlily.

"Who knows," said Petunia.

Junebug knew. She lived in the library and had read 1,872 books so far.

"Sesame is a flowering plant. It grows in tropical regions and is cultivated for its edible seeds, which grow in pods."

"Oh. Thank you, Junebug, that's interesting," said Violet. "But how are we going to find VEGETABLE seeds? If we don't show up with seeds tomorrow, I just know that Miss Poppy will send us right back to Buttercups!"

Tigerlily remembered seeing some seed packets in the shed, where she and her family spent summer vacations. Tigerlily loved the cool dirt floors and sleeping in nests on the sweet-smelling grass they brought in from outside. It was almost like camping. Tigerlily had spent hours exploring the lawn mowers and bicycle tires. In fact, exploring the shed would be much more fun than gardening.

"I've got an idea," said Tigerlily. "Follow me."

The Scouts followed Tigerlily down
the sidewalk and across the street. They
scurried into Tigerlily's shed, squeaking
in delight. There was so much to see that
they almost forgot what they were there

for. On the floor next to a watering can and a coiled-up hose was a gardening basket. "This looks promising!" said Violet, climbing into the basket with Petunia and Hyacinth close behind. There were

tools, a roll of twine, and some gloves inside but no seeds. "Oh no!" said Violet. "Now what are we going to do?"

"Relax!" said Tigerlily from under a bench. "Look what I found!"

Tigerlily dragged crumpled seed packages into the open. They looked like trash, but when she opened one, there were still seeds in it. "Jackpot!" she said.

"I'm starved," said Cricket, pulling something out of her backpack. "Does anyone want some cheese?"

The Mouse Scouts pulled their sit-upons out of their backpacks and gathered in a circle. Cricket broke the cheese into six pieces and passed it around.

"Nothing says snack like Monterey Jack!" said Tigerlily.

Nothing says SNACK like Monterey JACK!

"None for me," said Junebug. "I'm lactose-intolerant."

The rest of the Scouts nibbled happily. The shed was quiet except for a strange rumbling that sounded almost like . . . purring!

Tigerlily looked
up and listened, her
whiskers quivering.
Sure enough, high on
a shelf, there was a
sleeping cat. Tigerlily
didn't trust cats, even
sleeping ones. "Cat!"
she whispered to the
other Scouts. "Run!"

"Don't forget the seeds!" squeaked
Violet.

MOUSE SCOUT HANDBOOK

FINDING AND CHOOSING SEEDS FOR YOUR VEGETABLE GARDEN

Cherry Tomato   Mouse Scout   Regular Tomato

Before you plant your garden, you must decide which plants you would like to grow. Try to choose vegetables that you can easily carry.

Pumpkin

Carrot   Radish   Pea Pod   String Bean

Corn, squash, eggplants, and tomatoes, while delicious, are very unwieldy. Peas, beans, radishes, cherry tomatoes, baby beets, and carrots are a better choice for the gardening Acorn Scout.

If you are lucky enough to live near humans who garden, seeds will be easily found in the garage or garden shed. Seed packets

A single pea
is a healthy snack.

do not weigh much, but they are bulky. If you plan on taking the entire packet, it is best to have some other mice with you. You may want to tear open a corner of the packet and take just what you need. Be sure that the seeds are labeled so you know what they are. Bird feeders are another source of seeds, but with those you may be limited to a garden of sunflowers and corn.

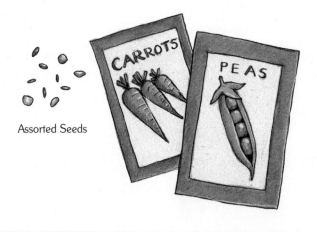

Assorted Seeds

CHAPTER 4

Nothing but Dirt

Bright and early the next morning, the Mouse Scouts met outside of the Left Meadow Elementary School with their seed packets. Violet handed out gardening gloves she had made the night before from an old sock. She had found it one day, bunched behind the dryer in the laundry room of the house where she lived, and knew it would come in handy.

Junebug was covered head to toe in mosquito netting. "It's a precaution," she said.

"From what?" asked Tigerlily.

"Bugs, mites, sun, dust, and pollen," said Junebug. "I have sensitivities."

Miss Poppy instructed them to get some gardening tools out of the utensil bin in

the cafeteria. When they came back outside, she led them to a weedy corner of
the playground.

"This will be our GARDEN," she said.
"Before we get started, a few words. Gardening is not all sunshine and straw-
berries. It is hard WORK. You have to
clear the plot of weeds, roots, and rocks.

Achoo!

By the time you are done, I don't want to see ANYTHING. Not a dandelion. Not a blade of grass. Not a pebble. Nothing but DIRT."

The Mouse Scouts got to work pulling out weeds and raking the soil with their gardening forks. It was hot, itchy, hard work. "I knew I wouldn't like this," Tigerlily muttered. But Violet was determined. She wasn't going to let mean old Miss Poppy or a little hard work bother her. She was an Acorn Scout, and they were creating the garden of her dreams. It was going to be wonderful, she just knew it!

Finally, the garden was cleared. "Not bad, for new Acorns," Miss Poppy admitted as she bent down to pick up a tiny pebble. "But it's not a garden until we plant something. Let's see your seeds."

The Scouts lined up their seed packets.

"Oh my!" Miss Poppy said. "Cherry tomatoes! Beans! Peas! Carrots! Radishes! Brussels sprouts! Each of you will pick a seed packet to plant. That vegetable will be your responsibility."

"Brussels sprouts?" moaned Tigerlily.

I HATE Brussels sprouts.

"I hate Brussels sprouts."

"I love them," said Hyacinth. "My mother always serves them at our elegant dinner parties."

She lived in a dollhouse in the mayor's attic and had a beautiful dining room. Her mother loved to show it off.

"Good," said Tigerlily. "You can have them."

Next the Scouts dug trenches and carefully planted their seeds. Violet found some sticks and put one at the end of each row with a seed packet on it so they could tell what they had planted where. Then they watered the garden.

"Good work, Scouts," said Miss Poppy. "Weekly Scout meetings will continue through the summer, along with your garden commitments. I will make frequent inspections of the garden, so be sure to keep on top of it. And REMEMBER: A garden takes care and patience. You have to WATER the garden. It cannot be too DRY. It cannot be too WET. There will be PESTS. Always wear sunscreen. Keep hydrated. You will get DIRTY. Don't pick vegetables before they are ready. Do not allow the vegetables to get too big. Beware of POISON IVY. And don't forget . . . HAVE FUN!"

With that, Miss Poppy left the garden.

The Mouse Scouts gathered their tools and admired their work.

"What a beautiful garden!" said Violet.

"It's nothing but dirt," said Tigerlily. "When does the growing start?"

MOUSE SCOUT HANDBOOK

PREPARING AND PLANTING
THE GARDEN

Your garden will be a wonderful spot to spend summer days. Be sure to pick a place that is sunny and has rich soil. There should be water nearby.

Tools: Recycled plastic forks and spoons make excellent tools for turning over the soil, raking, and weeding. Small combs also come in handy for raking the soil.

SPOON
for scraping
and scooping

FORK
for raking
and digging

GRAPEFRUIT
SPOON
for cutting
through
stubborn roots

CHOPSTICKS
for planting
seeds and
staking
tall plants

COMB
for fine raking

Dirt: Once you have chosen the perfect spot for your garden, you will need to clear it of all weeds, roots, and rocks. Turn the soil over with a fork or spoon to loosen it, then rake smooth, taking care not to compact the soil. Water generously and let the soil rest awhile before planting.

Planting: Now that your soil is ready, it is time to plant the seeds. Dig a trench with your spoon. Carefully place seeds in the trench one at a time, about an inch apart. When you are done, cover with soil and rake smooth. Water again. Before you know it, you will see sprouts and your garden will be growing!

CHAPTER 5

‿

Sprouts

It was really too soon for any real work to be done in the garden, but Violet checked on it every day just the same. Each week at the Mouse Scout meeting, she reported on the status. "No growth yet."

"Patience!" Miss Poppy would reply. "Keep monitoring it."

Violet blushed. She had never felt so important before.

Then one day, Violet noticed that the

garden looked dry. *Someone should probably water it*, she thought. Then she remembered something she had read in the *Mouse Scout Handbook* about doing things that needed to be done without having to be told. "Oh. I guess *I* could water it!"

Violet looked at the hose. It had been hard enough to lift it with *all* of the Scouts. She would never be able to do it herself. Maybe Tigerlily could help.

Violet found Tigerlily sliding down the drainpipe by her house. "There you are!" said Tigerlily. "You're missing all the fun."

Violet shuddered. She was not fond of drainpipes. Spiders liked to hide in them.

"I need your help watering the garden," Violet said.

"I'll help you tomorrow if you'll slide with me today," said Tigerlily. "It's not like anything is growing yet anyway."

Violet wasn't sure. The garden had looked *awfully* dry. But maybe Tigerlily was right. Another day probably wouldn't make any difference. And she had been so busy monitoring the garden, she hadn't played with Tigerlily in a while.

"Oh, all right. I guess it can wait one more day," said Violet as she climbed up the drainpipe. When she got to the top, she closed her eyes, took a deep breath, and, with a *whoosh*, slid down the drainpipe. It was more fun than she expected. She climbed up again, and she and Tigerlily spent the rest of the afternoon sliding down the drainpipe. Violet forgot all about the garden.

When Violet got to the garden the next morning, she saw a few little sprouts lying flat on the ground. "They're dying of thirst!" she cried. "I knew I should have watered them yesterday. I am a *terrible gardener*!" Violet sank to the ground and buried her face in her

hands. "It's over before it even began."
She wallowed in misery.

While Violet was wallowing, Tigerlily
arrived, rolling a large plastic water bottle in front of her. She used her claws to
make little holes in the plastic. Then she

climbed on top of the bottle. Violet stood up and wiped her eyes. "Tigerlily, what are you doing? You said you would help me water the garden. This is no time for games." Tigerlily just smiled and began to jump up and down on the bottle. Water started squirting out of the sides.

"Oh," said Violet. "Nice sprinkler!"

"Thanks!" said Tigerlily. "It will work even better if we both jump on it."

Violet was skeptical. She wanted the garden watered, but jumping on the bottle looked dangerous. Still, Tigerlily did have a point. Violet sighed and climbed up on the bottle and tentatively started jumping. It was sort of scary . . . and sort of fun. Until the bottle got slippery and she slid off.

"Ouch!" Violet squeaked. She was

about to get mad at Tigerlily when she saw that the little green sprouts were already starting to perk up. Maybe the garden was going to make it after all!

At the next Mouse Scout meeting, Violet reported that the garden was growing.

She swelled with pride as she described their watering efforts, making sure to give Tigerlily credit for her sprinkler invention.

"Thank you, Violet," said Miss Poppy. "We all appreciate your hard work, but remember, this is a *Mouse Scout* garden. Everyone has her own vegetable to look after. In addition, we need to monitor the garden so it's tidy, weedless, and watered regularly. I've made this Duty Chart to make sure that everyone pitches in. Be sure to sign in before going outside."

The Scouts each filled in her name and headed out to the garden. Cricket thinned the carrots, and Junebug thinned the radishes. Tigerlily untangled the beanstalks.

Petunia made stakes for the cherry tomatoes out of coffee stirrers, and Hyacinth dusted every little Brussels sprout. Violet made a trellis out of pencils for the peas. Soon everything was in order. It was beginning to look like a real garden.

~~~~~~~~~~~~~~~~~~~~~~~~~~~

MAKING A DUTY CHART

One of the great joys of Mouse Scouting is working together on group projects. But working together takes organization! Otherwise, some mice might find themselves doing all of the work while other mice linger on the sidelines. Creating a Duty Chart is a helpful way to divide labor and make sure that each mouse gets a part in the project.

Making a Duty Chart is easy and fun. First, make a list of all of the tasks that need to be done. Decide whether a task should be handled by a group or by an individual.

Next, decide on the style of chart that will work best for you. It can be a grid, a wheel, a table, or whatever you like. Creative and eye-catching charts are always fun and help to spark enthusiasm for the task at hand.

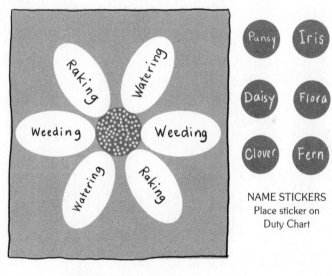

NAME STICKERS
Place sticker on
Duty Chart

FLOWER DUTY CHART

One of the most important aspects of the Duty Chart is to rotate duties so that every Scout has a chance to work at each task. If the Scouts are working in small groups, be sure to rotate partners so that each Scout has a chance to work with somebody new.

With planning and teamwork, even the most difficult tasks can be completed with success.

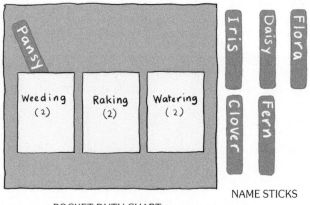

POCKET DUTY CHART

NAME STICKS

Next, decide on the style of chart that will work best for you. It can be a grid, a wheel, a table, or whatever you like. Creative and eye-catching charts are always fun and help to spark enthusiasm for the task at hand.

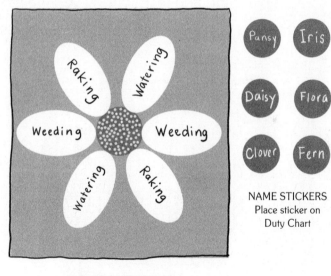

FLOWER DUTY CHART

NAME STICKERS
Place sticker on
Duty Chart

One of the most important aspects of the Duty Chart is to rotate duties so that every Scout has a chance to work at each task. If the Scouts are working in small groups, be sure to rotate partners so that each Scout has a chance to work with somebody new.

With planning and teamwork, even the most difficult tasks can be completed with success.

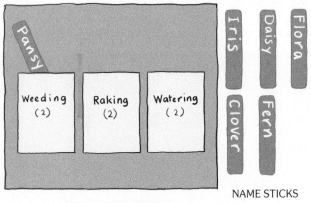

POCKET DUTY CHART

NAME STICKS

CHAPTER 6

❦

Bugs, Slugs, and Grubs

After that, the garden was a hubbub of activity. There was always someone there, weeding or watering or tending to her vegetable. Sometimes Violet missed the peaceful days when she was the only one who visited, but it was nice to see things getting done.

One day, when Violet got to the garden, it seemed even livelier than usual. Not only were Petunia and Hyacinth busily weeding the cherry tomatoes and the Brussels sprouts, there was other activity as well. Bees were buzzing around the cherry tomato blossoms, ladybugs were feasting on aphids, and earthworms were wriggling beneath her feet. Violet was so surprised that she almost walked into a spiderweb. "Watch where you're going. I've been working on this all morning," called a voice from the web, and Violet jumped when she saw a huge spider. She swallowed and said, "Thank you, everyone, for your hard work." She had read in her *Mouse Scout Handbook* that some worms and insects could be very helpful to the garden.

Violet was just admiring how nicely her peas were climbing the trellis when she noticed that some of the leaves had been chewed. *That's funny,* she thought. *Maybe it was Cricket? She'll eat anything.* But then she heard a *Chomp! Chomp! Chomp!,* which didn't sound like Cricket at all. It was coming from under one of the leaves. Violet took a deep breath and lifted the leaf. There was a weevil, busily eating his way through a pea!

"Hey!" the weevil shouted. "Do you mind? I'm eating."

"Sorry!" Violet squeaked. She ran to find Hyacinth by the Brussels sprouts, but Hyacinth was having problems of her own.

"What is *that*?" she asked Violet, pointing to a slug. "It looks like some kind of giant booger."

Petunia looked over from the cherry tomatoes and started laughing. But her laugh turned into a squeal as a flea beetle hopped from a tomato leaf and landed on her acorn cap. *"Get it off me!"* Petunia ran to Hyacinth, and Hyacinth started squealing, too.

"This garden is infested!" Hyacinth wailed. She raced out of the garden, with Petunia close behind.

"Wait for me!" Violet tried to run after them, but she tripped on a pea vine and crashed to the ground. She felt something squirming over her nose and opened her eyes to see a grub. She batted at the grub and scrambled to her feet.

All around her, Violet heard crunching and buzzing. And it seemed that every-where she looked there were grubs, bugs, and slugs. The garden was being eaten alive. Behind her, she heard something rustling. It sounded bigger than a bug and meaner than a grub. And then that some-thing tapped her on the shoulder.

Violet screamed!

She turned around and there was Miss
Poppy. "This garden is not a playground,"
said Miss Poppy. "I hope you are taking it
seriously enough to earn your 'Sow It and
Grow It' badge."

"Yes, Miss Poppy," Violet squeaked as
she ran out of the garden.

MOUSE SCOUT HANDBOOK

FRIENDS AND ENEMIES OF THE GARDEN

Garden Friends

As you work in your garden, remember that you are not the only one who works there. You have many helpers. Below are just a few of your gardening friends!

Bees: Bees are important friends of the gardener. They pollinate flowers, which enables plants to grow fruits and vegetables. They also use pollen to make honey, so if you see a bee, do not bother her. She is very busy.

Earthworms: You might think you don't like worms, but if you want to be a gardener, think again! Earthworms help to create drainage in the garden by making small tunnels in the ground. They eat soil and decaying matter. As these pass through the body, certain chemical reactions take place that help to fertilize the garden.

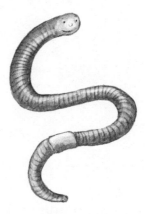

Ladybugs: Ladybugs are not only cute but also very helpful in the garden. Ladybugs love to eat aphids. Aphids are small insects that destroy plants by sucking sap from their stems.

Spiders: Spiders build beautiful webs, but those webs are more than just decoration. Spiders also trap harmful insects in their webs. They get a good dinner, and your plants are saved from the dangers of the insects.

Garden Foes

Not everyone in the garden is a friend. At one time or another, you will come across some pests that see your garden as their favorite lunch spot. Below are a few to be on the lookout for.

Weevils: Weevils are small beetles that love to eat the leaves and flowers of plants. There are thousands of varieties.

Slugs: Slugs are slimy creatures that are actually snails without shells. They love to eat leaves and flowers. A small slug can eat as much as twice its weight in one night.

Flea beetles: Flea beetles are tiny beetles that  hop like fleas when they are disturbed. If left alone, they enjoy eating the leaves of plants.

Grubs: Grubs are the larvae of various beetles. They live beneath the soil and feed on roots.

CHAPTER 7

Tigerlily Fights Back

Violet ran from the garden right into Tigerlily. She had never been so happy to see her friend.

"Tigerlily, help!" Violet gasped. "Miss Poppy! Oh, it's horrible! It's a *disaster*!"

"*What's* a disaster?" Tigerlily asked. "*What's* horrible? Besides Miss Poppy, I mean."

"There are *bugs*!" Violet gasped. "And *grubs*! And *slugs*!"

"Grubs? Bugs? Slugs?" asked Tigerlily. "In the *garden*?" Tigerlily was intrigued. Gardening was turning out to be much more interesting than she had imagined.

"This calls for action. Wait here, I'll be right back," Tigerlily said.

In a few minutes, Tigerlily returned, pulling a rattling wagon behind her.

"What is *that*?" Violet asked.

"It's my emergency wagon. I've got all of my handiest tools in here. I'll take care of those pests in no time!"

"I hope you're right." Violet couldn't imagine what Tigerlily had in mind, but then Tigerlily was always surprising her.

When they arrived at the garden, Tigerlily got to work. She pulled a wooden spoon out of the wagon and began

batting the tomato leaves with it. Flea beetles went flying. One landed in the spiderweb. "Hey, thanks for lunch!" the spider called out.

"No problem!" said Tigerlily, swinging the spoon. One beetle clung to a leaf for dear life, but it was too much for him. He fell to the ground and scuttled away.

Tigerlily handed the spoon to Violet, and Violet started batting the beanstalks. Then Tigerlily took out a toothpick and poked at the slug.

"Ouch!" said the slug. "What are you doing?"

"Get off that plant or I'll poke you again," Tigerlily said. "But next time will be harder."

"No!" cried the slug. "I'm delicate! I'm leaving, I'm leaving! Please don't poke me!" The slug slithered off as fast as it could (which wasn't very fast at all), leaving a trail of slime.

Next, Tigerlily went to the pea vines. She took off her Mouse Scout neck scarf and laid it flat on the ground beneath the vines. Then she gently shook the vines, and

I might need a new scarf!

the weevils fell to the ground. Tigerlily quickly bundled up her scarf and shook it out at the far end of the playground. "I might need a new scarf!" she said.

No Bugs,
Slugs,
or
Grubs!

Finally, the garden was free of pests. To be sure none would return, Violet made a sign and posted it at the entry to the garden.

Tigerlily took a look around. The garden was a little battered, but she couldn't believe how much it had grown.

The pea pods were getting plump, there were small green tomatoes, and beans were practically growing before her eyes. Tigerlily took a bean and bit into it. "This is delicious!" she said.

This is DELICIOUS!

MOUSE SCOUT HANDBOOK

THE PEST-FREE GARDEN

Keeping Pests Out of the Garden

Now that your vegetable garden is growing, suddenly everyone is interested in it. But not everyone is welcome. Below are a few safe and easy tricks for getting rid of unwelcome guests.

Slugs: Slugs love melon even more than your plants. Leave melon rinds around the garden in the evening and take them away in the morning, slugs and all.

Slugs will also collect in empty flowerpots.

Spread pet hair around plants. Slugs hate it!

Weevils, aphids, and beetles: It may be tedious, but an effective way to get rid of pests on your plants is to pick them off by hand. Be sure to have a pail of soapy water nearby to drop them in.

You can also place a cloth on the ground and gently bat at plants with a wooden spoon. The pests will fall from the plants onto the cloth. Shake the cloth far away from the garden.

The very best way to get rid of pests is to let others do the work for you. Turtles, toads, and salamanders love to eat slugs, beetles, and other insects. Make them feel at home by placing small rocks and piles of wood around your garden. Birds also love slugs, bugs, and grubs. Leave a collection of nest-building materials near your garden to encourage them to set up home there.

CHAPTER 8

❧

Vegetable Thieves

The next day, Tigerlily could barely sit through the Mouse Scout meeting. She was excited to get back to the garden. She was ready in case any of the pests had dared to come back. Violet was just relieved that the pest problem had been taken care of.

But when they finally got to the garden, neither of them was prepared for what they found. It looked as if a tornado had

touched down. Carrots had been ripped
out of the ground. Empty pea pods were
littered everywhere. The sign that Violet had made was pulled up and tossed
aside. Someone had taken a bite out of
each tomato.

"This is even worse than before!"

moaned Violet. "Instead of getting rid of the pests, we just made them angry."

"No slug or weevil could do this much damage," said Tigerlily. "It had to be something bigger."

"How much bigger?" Violet's whiskers quivered.

Just then, they heard something crashing through the tomato plants and looked up to see a thuggish rabbit running off with a radish. There was another rustle by the beans. A chipmunk took a bite of

a small Brussels sprout and spit it out. "Yuck. I hate Brussels sprouts," he said, tossing it to the squirrel next to him.

"Thanks! I love 'em," said the squirrel. "Try the carrots. They're pretty good."

"Yum. You missed the party last night." The chipmunk laughed. "We were bowling with peas. It was hilarious."

"Let's do it again tonight," the rabbit said. "And we should invite the raccoons. They're always up for a good time!"

"It's a plan!" said the squirrel.

The animals crashed out of the garden, trampling plants on their way.

Violet was devastated. The garden was a mess. Again.

"I give up," Violet said to Tigerlily. "We may have been able to get rid of the little pests, but we are no match for wild animals. All of our hard work was for nothing."

"Come on, Violet," said Tigerlily. "We'll think of something."

"What can we do?" asked Violet. "We are just little mice. It's no use. I'm going home."

We're more than mice. We're MOUSE SCOUTS!

"You're wrong, Violet," Tigerlily called after her. "We're more than mice. We're MOUSE SCOUTS! We can come up with a plan."

But Violet just kept walking.

MOUSE SCOUT HANDBOOK

BEWARE

OF VEGETABLE THIEVES

As if beetles, weevils, slugs, and grubs weren't bad enough, there are other garden intruders to be aware of. Most animals love vegetables, especially when someone else is doing all of the work. Here are a few to be especially on the lookout for.

WANTED
FOR
TRESPASSING, THEFT
&
GENERAL MAYHEM

Rabbits: Known for taking carrots, they also love lettuce and radishes.

Squirrels: Love to sample a wide variety of vegetables without finishing any of them.

Chipmunks: Love to burrow in gardens, nibbling on carrots, radishes, and other roots along the way.

Raccoons: Have no respect for the hard work of others. They love to dig in the garden, enjoy trampling plants, and will eat everything.

CHAPTER 9

Tigerlily Takes a Stand

"Even if Violet has given up on the garden, I'm not going to." Tigerlily clenched her jaw and balled her paws. "We're Mouse Scouts. We can handle thick and thin. We might be tall, but we can plan. We are strong . . . and in need. We have the power of, um, the oak tree." Tigerlily hadn't memorized the pledge or the song yet, but she knew there was something about acorns and oak trees and power and strength.

Tigerlily set off for the park to find the other Scouts. It didn't take long. Hyacinth and Petunia were sunbathing in the sandbox. Cricket was wading in the birdbath.

Junebug was reading the ingredients on a crumpled bag of Cheeso Delights. "Sodium diacetate? Disodium guanylate? How could anyone eat this? There are more chemicals and preservatives than actual ingredients!" She put on her gardening gloves and dragged the bag over to the trash can.

"Scouts, listen up," Tigerlily said. The Scouts gathered around her.

"What's going on?" asked Cricket.

"We've got a problem in the garden."

"I thought you took care of those bugs," said Hyacinth, flicking a grain of sand from her nose.

"This is a bigger problem." Tigerlily told them all about the animals.

"Those animals are a nuisance. Someone should do something," said Petunia.

"Yes, someone should," said Junebug. "Who knows how many diseases they've spread through the garden already."

"*We* should do something," Tigerlily said.

"What can *we* do?" said Cricket, nibbling on a Cheeso Delight that had fallen out of Junebug's bag. "We're not exactly the toughest rodents on the block. Mmm, these are *delicious*!"

"We may be small, but we can be tough when we have to be," said Tigerlily. "What is the one animal an elephant fears?"

Everyone just stared at her.

"A mouse!" shouted Tigerlily. "What animal has helped humans make important leaps in medicine and the other sciences?"

"The mouse!" said Junebug. She was extremely proud of the fact that her parents were retired lab mice.

"What animal can make a human scream and jump on a chair just by running across a floor?"

"A MOUSE!" everyone joined in.

"Do any of those mice back down when the going gets tough?" Tigerlily asked. "NO! And neither do we. Why?"

"BECAUSE WE'RE MOUSE SCOUTS!" Everyone cheered.

"So what are we going to do?" asked Junebug when the cheering had died down.

Everyone looked at Tigerlily. Tigerlily had no idea what to do.

"We've got to take them by surprise," Violet said. "And we've got to scare them. Scare them so badly that they never want to come back."

"Good thinking, Violet," said Tigerlily. "What could be scary enough to scare scary animals?"

Nobody said anything.

"Come on, Scouts. Think!" said Tigerlily. "What are *you* afraid of?"

Violet shut her eyes tightly and tried to think of the very scariest thing that she could imagine. She had been scared plenty of times, but there was one thing that scared her more than any other.

"I know," Violet said. She whispered it in Tigerlily's ear.

"That's it!" Tigerlily shouted. She told everyone Violet's idea and gave them a list of things to bring to the garden.

MOUSE SCOUT HANDBOOK

VERBENA · HEPATICA · ASTER

FAMOUS MICE IN HISTORY

Verbena: Legend has it that in ancient times, an elephant carelessly ruined Verbena's home by stepping on it. Verbena took revenge by running up the inside of the elephant's trunk. The elephant nearly suffocated before Verbena ran back down the trunk. From that day on, elephants have feared mice.

Hepatica: In the early 1950s, Hepatica led a team of research mice who, working closely with scientists, developed the first successful vaccine for polio. Not one to rest on her laurels, Hepatica founded the Research Institute for Mice (RIM), which has since become the foremost center for mice aspiring to enter the medical research profession.

Aster: On a fall day in 1972, a young Mouse Scout named Aster was searching the kitchen floor for crumbs when a thief broke in. On seeing Aster, the thief screamed and jumped on a chair. Aster fought her urge to run and hide and stayed in the kitchen, keeping the thief on the chair until the humans returned home. Sadly, the humans never recognized Aster for her feat, but Mouse Scouts celebrate her bravery with a crumb feast each fall.

CHAPTER 10

The Plan

Tigerlily was the first to arrive at the garden. She had four pencils. She poked two of them into the sides of her plastic-water-bottle sprinkler and two into the bottom.

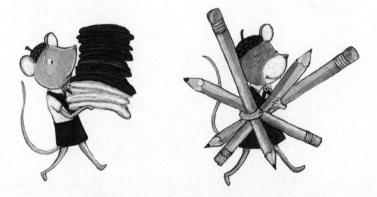

Violet was close behind her with a bundle of cloth. "This was the best I could do." She unrolled the bundle to reveal a few squares of green cloth and a white handkerchief. She and Tigerlily draped them over the water bottle and fiddled with it. "Not bad," said Tigerlily when they were done.

Then Hyacinth and Petunia showed up rolling a foam football.

"That's perfect," said Tigerlily. She and Violet hoisted the football onto the top of the water bottle.

Cricket was next, dragging a beret behind her. "This has been in the store's lost-and-found for months. No one will miss it."

Tigerlily put the beret on the football.

"We're just about ready," Tigerlily said. "Now all we have to do is stand it up."

Tigerlily dug two holes in the ground, then lassoed a shoelace around the bottle. The Scouts pulled the laces until the bottle was standing upright, supported by the two pencils on the bottom. Tigerlily eased the ends of the pencils into the holes that she had dug and then let go. The bottle stood on its own.

"That's a pretty impressive scarecrow," Cricket said.

"Something is missing," said Hyacinth.

Just then, Junebug came running into the garden, dragging a pair of eyeglasses behind her. "People are always leaving these at the library."

Tigerlily climbed up the scarecrow, and the Scouts lifted the glasses up to her. She placed them on the football.

When they were done, Violet looked carefully at the scarecrow. It certainly

looked scary, but something still wasn't quite right.

"Come on, Violet, I think they're coming!" Tigerlily called from behind the Scouts' hiding place in the Brussels sprouts. Violet slipped behind the Brussels sprouts just as the animals came bounding into the garden.

"The radishes are tasty," they heard the rabbit say to the chipmunk. "I'm going to dig up the rest of— *Aaargh!*"

"What *is* that?" asked the chipmunk.

"I don't know, but it looks kind of funny," said the squirrel. "I wonder what it's doing here."

"It will make a great target," said the chipmunk, throwing a pea at the scarecrow. The other animals laughed and began throwing peas, too.

Violet couldn't believe it! They had worked so hard on the scarecrow. How dare those animals make fun of it? *How could they not be afraid of it?* she wondered. And then it struck Violet just what was missing from the scarecrow. Violet felt for her emergency whistle, which was hanging around her neck. She brought it up to her mouth and blew as hard as she could.

"THWEEEEEEEEEEEEEEEEET!"

The chipmunk froze and looked around. "What was that?" he asked. All of the animals looked a bit frightened.

The other Scouts reached for their whistles, and everyone blew. Together, they made a terrible screeching sound.

"Ow, my ears!" yelled the rabbit.

"Let's get out of here," said the squirrel, and they all ran off, covering their ears.

The Scouts cheered. And then they got to work. There were vegetables to harvest.

MOUSE SCOUT HANDBOOK

YOUR EMERGENCY WHISTLE

One of the most important things in a Mouse Scout's possession is her emergency whistle. Your emergency whistle alerts other Scouts to danger and can also call them to your aid. Only use your whistle in times of true emergency, and even then, use it sparingly. The whistle is piercingly loud, and prolonged exposure to loud tweets has been known to cause ear damage.

How to use your emergency whistle: Once you have determined that you are faced with a true emergency, draw the whistle to your lips and blow into it. The duration and sequence of your tweets will depend on the nature of your emergency.

When the emergency whistle should be used:

- You are lost.
- There is a large animal threatening you or another animal that can't defend itself.
- You are caught in a mousetrap.

-THWEET!-

Remember: Your emergency whistle is not a toy. It should be used only in cases of true emergency.

The Badge Ceremony

The Mouse Scout garden was a success. Violet's peas had been destroyed in the animals' bowling match, but the other vegetables had done well. Nothing was as successful as the Brussels sprouts, much to Tigerlily's dismay—and Hyacinth's delight. Miss Poppy announced that the badges would be awarded in the garden.

When the garden was weeded and raked, the Scouts made a display of their vegetables in the center.

"Just in time!" said Violet. "Here comes Miss Poppy now!"

"Uh-oh. We forgot something." Tiger-lily looked over at the Miss Poppy scarecrow. "Do you think she'll notice?"

And then Miss Poppy did a surprising thing. She smiled. "Well done, Mouse Scouts. Well done."

MOUSE SCOUT HANDBOOK

THE "SOW IT AND GROW IT" BADGE

To earn this badge, you must complete at least five of the following activities:

1. Clear a plot of land for a garden.

2. Obtain seeds to plant in the garden.

3. Plant seeds and raise healthy plants by making sure they are watered and weeded regularly.

4. Be able to identify at least three different weeds.

5. Be able to identify at least three different garden pests.

6. Learn to keep your garden safe from other animals.

7. Successfully grow at least one type of vegetable.

8. Enjoy your vegetable harvest by preparing at least one recipe per vegetable.

MOUSE SCOUT BADGES

Sow It and Grow It

Mouse Scout Heritage

Fun with Foraging

Make a Difference

Baking with Seeds

Take Flight

Dramatics

Signs of Fall

First Aid

Winter Safety

Predator Awareness

Camp Out

Flower Fashions

Weaving with Grass

The Night Sky

Friendship

THE ACORN SCOUT SONG

Melody by Frank Fighera

We are A – corns, ti – ny and small. But
we'll grow up to be migh – ty and tall. We're
quick with a plan, and we help when we can. We
love our friends and are kind to all.